I Wish My Brother Was a Dog

Carol Diggory Shields

Illustrated by Paul Meisel

ORCHARD BOOKS
96 Leonard Street, London EC2A 4RH
Orchard Books Australia
14 Mars Road, Lane Cove, NSW 2066
ISBN 1 86039 598 8 (hardback)
ISBN 1 86039 632 1 (paperback)
First published in the United States 1997
by Dutton Children's Books,
a division of Penguin Books USA Inc.
First published in Great Britain 1997
First paperback publication 1998

1 2 3 4 5 6 02 01 00 99 98 97

Printed in Belgium

For David and Sally, with love – C.D.S.

For my brothers, Jim, Gary and Ron,
and for the real dog, Taffy – P.M.

I wish my brother was a dog!

MY ROCKS
8
Danger
MYTOYS
Do NOT TOUCH
This means U!
BUZZBALL
BUZZBALL
BINGO RAMA
ZING ZANG

Andy, I'd like you a lot better if you were a dog.

If you were a dog, I'd buy you some dog toys with my pocket money. A chewy bone and lots of bouncy balls. You could play with them all the time and never, never, *never* touch my toys again.

Andy, you'd have a lot more hair if you were a dog.
And a lot more teeth, too. Then you could be a watchdog!
You could stay at home and guard the house when Mum
and I go out. All by ourselves. See you later, Andy!

NO
DOGS
ALLOWED
BINKY
ANDY

Andy, if you were a dog, you wouldn't always be smushing your peas and squishing your applesauce and making a big mess at the table. You'd get to eat out of a nice red bowl with your name on it, on the kitchen floor. Andy's a good name for a dog.

Tricks, Andy! Dogs can do tricks! I could teach you to shake hands and beg and jump through a hoop. And we could play games like fetch and tug-of-war and Frisbee.

We wouldn't have to listen to you cry anymore. If you were a dog, you could bark instead. And if you got too loud, we'd put you outside on the back steps.

You wouldn't have to sleep in my room in that squeaky old crib anymore, either. If you were a dog, you could sleep in the hall. Or we could build you a little house, just the right size – way, way out in the back garden.

Just think, Andy, if you were a dog,
no more stinky nappies.

You could play out in the garden all afternoon if you were a dog. Dig holes and chase squirrels and roll in the mud. You wouldn't need a bath. We'd wash you off with a hose.

If you didn't feel good, we wouldn't fuss and worry and carry you around and say, "Poor little baby-waby." We'd take you to a vet, and he'd give you an injection.

WIN THE
WAR AGAINST
FLEAS

And if Mum and Dad and I went somewhere, you wouldn't need to ride in your car seat in the back with me or stay at home with a grumpy baby-sitter. You could stay in a kennel.

If you were a dog, Andy, we could put you on a lead and take you to a dog show. You'd be the best dog there. You could show off all the tricks I taught you, and you might win a prize, Andy!

BEST
OF
BREED

And then somebody might want to buy you!

Good-bye, Andy.

It'll be really peaceful around here with no baby . . .
and no dog . . . and no disasters . . .

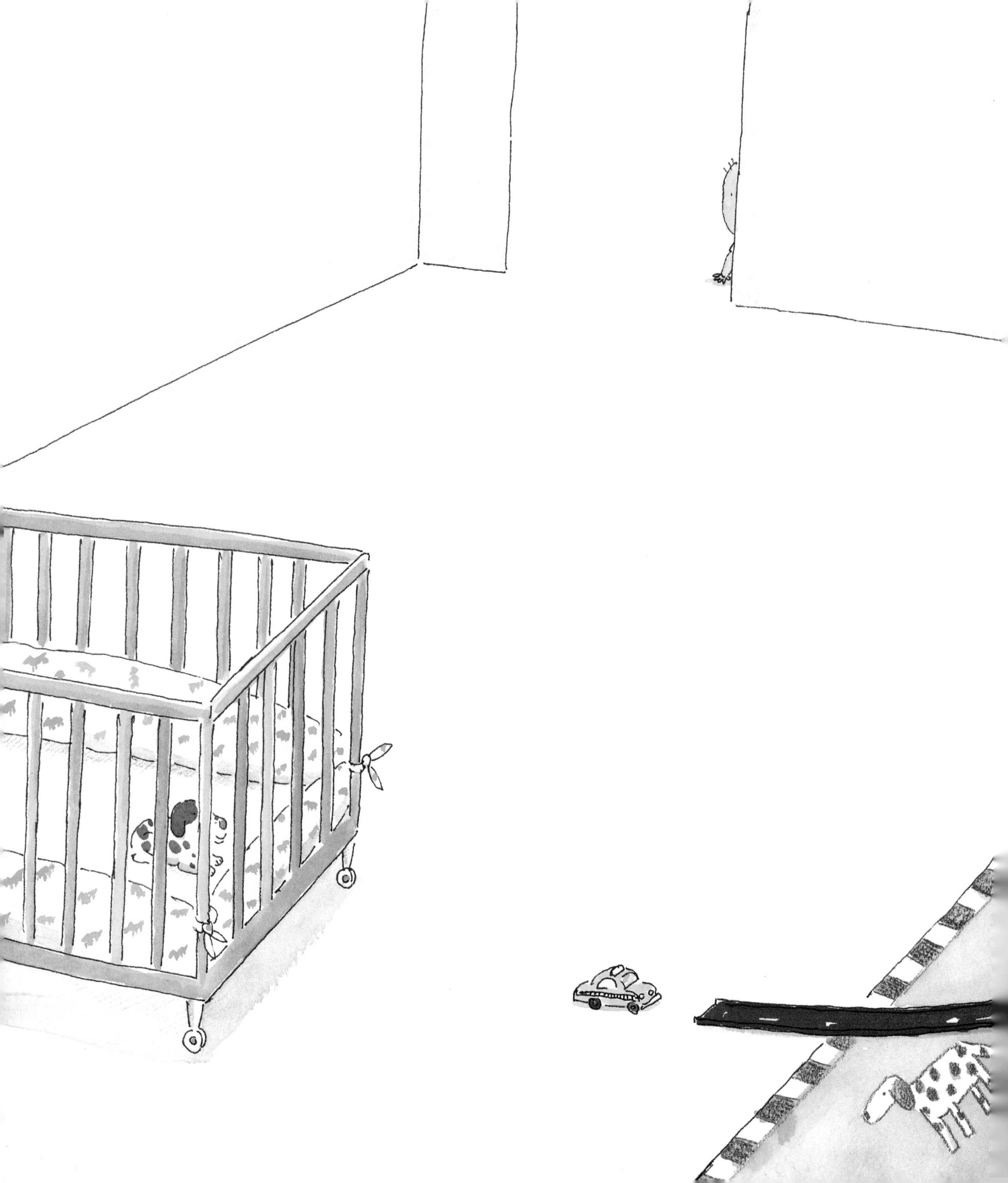

Too peaceful.

Maybe I'll just keep you, Andy, if Mum says it's okay.

You know what, Andy? If you were my dog, I'd take really good care of you. Most of the time I'd treat you like you were . . .

my very own brother.